Elliott Finds
a Clue

Elliott Finds a Clue

And Other Quicksolve Mini-Mysteries

Jim Sukach

Illustrated by Alan Flinn

Sterling Publishing Co., Inc.
New York

Quicksolve Mysteries™ is a trademark of James Richard Sukach.

Library of Congress Cataloging-in-Publication Data Available

10 9 8 7 6 5 4 3 2 1

Published by Sterling Publishing Co., Inc.
387 Park Avenue South, New York, NY 10016
© 2004 by James Richard Sukach
Distributed in Canada by Sterling Publishing
c/o Canadian Manda Group, One Atlantic Avenue, Suite 105
Toronto, Ontario, Canada M6K 3E7
Distributed in Great Britain by Chrysalis Books Group PLC
The Chrysalis Building, Bramley Road, London W10 6SP, England
Distributed in Australia by Capricorn Link (Australia) Pty. Ltd.
P.O. Box 704, Windsor, NSW 2756, Australia

Sterling ISBN 1-4027-1074-7

Contents

Dr. Jeffrey Lynn Quicksolve

Dr. J. L. Quicksolve is a professor of criminology who retired early from the police department, where he earned his reputation as a detective. Now he works with various police agencies and private detectives as a consultant when he's not teaching at the university.

He certainly knows his business, solving crimes. Many people are amazed at how he solves so many crimes so quickly. He says, "The more you know about people and the world we live in, the easier it is to solve a problem."

His son Junior enjoys learning too, and he solves a few mysteries himself. Join them in this book of Dr. Quicksolve mini-mysteries.

Then join the famous detective's humorous friend, Detective Elliott Savant, as he reveals his unusual knack for solving crimes while appearing oblivious to his surroundings. If you read carefully, think hard, and don't laugh too much, you can help them solve each case!

Gunshots in the Night

Dr. J. L. Quicksolve and his son Junior were spending a few days in New York City. Aunt Toni was traveling in Europe, but she let them stay in one of her large apartments on Broadway. They were on the ninth floor, and their apartment had a corner window that gave them a spectacular view of the brilliant, multi-colored, constantly flowing, flashing and blinking and rolling light show that erupted from Times Square.

They had started the day with breakfast at a small diner a block off Broadway. They shopped a little and walked around Central Park, where they waited in line for free tickets to "Shakespeare in the Park." They went down-town and had pizza in Little Italy and walked around until they got hungry again, then they had dinner in Chinatown after which they headed back uptown to the

Delacorte Theater in Central Park for the Shakespeare performance.

It was after midnight when they heard BAM! BAM! BAM! The sounds came echoing up through the canyons of the tall buildings.

"Gunshots!" Dr. Quicksolve said.

Junior ran to the window and looked down at the street below. "There are police cars at the end of our block," he said. Looking the other way, he said, "There are police cars at both ends. They're blocking the street. Do you suppose they're chasing somebody?"

Dr. Quicksolve climbed out of bed and went to the window. He stood beside his son and looked down.

"Look at the next block," he said.

Junior said, "Look at all those taxis!" There were no cars in front of their building, but Junior counted 14 taxis stopped on the next block. "Maybe they're searching the cabs for the gunman!" Junior said.

Suddenly the taxis all began to move. BAM! BAM! BAM! The sound of three shots rang out again. The taxis all stopped after traveling less than half a block. Strangely, they all backed up to their original positions.

"What is going on?" Junior said.

Again, the taxis moved forward. Again—BAM! BAM! BAM! Three shots rang out.

"Oh! I get it!" Dr. Quicksolve said.

What was happening on the street below in the middle of the night?

Answer on page 90.

Rescue Dog

D r. J. L. Quicksolve and his son Junior sat quietly in a small fishing boat. Their fishing lines disappeared into the glassy-smooth water. Junior slowly reeled in his line and cast it out toward the lily pads that blanketed the edge of the shoreline.

They liked getting out on the lake early in the morning before sunrise, but more importantly, they liked getting there before the roar of speed boats that later would crisscross the lake in frantic bedlam.

"Got one!" Junior said. He carefully reeled in his line, coaxing the struggling fish closer and closer to the boat and lifted up the bluegill, bringing it into the boat.

"When the motorboats and skiers start coming out,"

Dr. Quicksolve said, "we'll head in and take a look at that new puppy Ben told me he just brought home."

"I can't wait to see it," Junior said. "You said it's a Newfoundland?"

"That's right," his dad said. "Ben's worried about the kids in the families that rent his cabins. When he heard that Newfoundland dogs rescue people in the water the way St. Bernards rescue people in the snowy mountains, he decided to get one. The puppy will look like a St. Bernard, but be all black. He'll be a big, strong dog that likes the water."

"You said Ben is still trying to think of a name for the puppy?" Junior asked.

"That's right. Do you have any ideas?" Dr. Quicksolve asked.

"How about Spot?" Junior suggested. "If he's all black, he'll look like a big spot."

"That's a good idea," Dr. Quicksolve said, "but a Newfoundland is an awfully big spot!"

"Wait a minute!" Junior said. "I read about a man who rented boats and had a Newfoundland dog who rescued swimmers. He had the perfect name! Swimmers always called him when they were drowning!"

You should be able to guess that "perfect name!"

Answer on page 90.

Hit-and-Run

When Dr. Quicksolve approached the scene in his yellow VW Beetle, he could see an ambulance, two police cars, a man sitting on the ground being attended by two medics, and Officer Beekerjar from the police lab. Sergeant Rebekah Shurshot was standing by the police car. She walked over to greet Dr. Quicksolve when he parked along the road and got out of his car. "It's a hit-and-run," she said, getting right down to business.

Dr. Quicksolve walked over to the injured man, who was dressed in a running outfit and was sitting in the grass at the edge of the road. He seemed to be all right. Officer Beekerjar was examining the man's clothes with a magnifying glass. One of the medics came over to talk to Dr. Quicksolve and Sergeant Shurshot. "He was lucky. He said a silver Ford van hit him from behind. He heard it coming too late. He said he heard the wheels as they left the pavement and hit the gravel. He jumped just in time to avoid being run over. The minivan stopped for a minute and then took off. He got part of the license number." Officer Beekerjar handed a piece of paper to Sergeant Shurshot, who stepped aside to radio in a description of the vehicle.

Dr. Quicksolve and Sergeant Shurshot talked to the victim and Officer Beekerjar.

"I didn't hear the van until it was right on me," the injured runner said.

"You were jogging that way?" Sergeant Shurshot asked, pointing down the road.

"Yes. He hit me from behind and kept going that way after he stopped for a second," the man said.

"He's not hurt badly. The driver probably tried to stop. There's no sign of broken glass or paint or anything. The van probably isn't even damaged," Officer Beekerjar said.

"Let's go for a little ride that way," Dr. Quicksolve said to Sergeant Shurshot.

In Sergeant Shurshot's police car, they talked about what might have happened.

"Maybe the driver was drunk," Sergeant Shurshot suggested.

"Maybe he was just talking on his cell phone and not paying attention to his driving," Dr. Quicksolve said.

"Whatever happened, he's in big trouble now that he left the scene," Sergeant Shurshot said.

A radio message came, telling them that a suspicious van was discovered at a dealership three miles away. There was no damage, but the driver had arrived a short time earlier because his van had just blown a head gasket.

Dr. Quicksolve and Sergeant Shurshot arrived at the dealership and talked to the police officer who had found the van.

"The driver said he usually comes down the road where the hit-and-run took place, but today he went a different way to stop at a Slippery Oliver's Oil and Lube to get his oil changed. He said he got his oil changed and was on his way home when he saw a cloud of white
. smoke behind him. He realized it was coming from his

van and drove right to the dealership. He's complaining because the dealership said he's run past his warranty and he'll have to pay to get it fixed."

"Where's the van?" Dr. Quicksolve said.

"It's parked right there," the officer said, pointing to a silver van parked next to the building.

Dr. Quicksolve walked over to the van. He walked around it, checking the front end for damage. He bent over and cupped his hands around his eyes to look in through the windshield. Then he opened the door and looked at the windshield in front of the driver.

"Well," Dr. Quicksolve said. "It looks like he's lying about where he was."

What did Dr. Quicksolve find?

Answer on page 92.

Cardigan

Junior Quicksolve breathed out hard each time he pressed down strongly on the pedals of his bicycle—first one leg, then the other—in a smooth pumping cadence that was bringing him to the crest of a steep hill. He decided to stop at the top and rest while his friend Prissy Powers caught up with him. He came to a stop and sucked in a large gulp of fresh air as he turned his head to look back for his friend, who immediately raced past him, streaked over the crest, and headed straight down the steeply dropping slope of the other side of the hill before Junior realized what had happened. He pushed his bike forward and raced after her.

Prissy was sitting at a picnic table at the bottom of the hill near a stand of tall pine trees when Junior caught up to her. She already had their sandwiches out on the table.

"I love the way Jim Sukach writes your Dad's stories," Prissy told Junior.

"Especially when you're in the story, right?" Junior joked.

"I read another author's book of mini-mysteries the other day," Prissy said.

"Oh, no!" Junior said, smiling.

"It wasn't that good," she said.

"You weren't in it?" Junior chimed.

"Besides that," she said. "One story, for example, was about a woman who was carrying money from work to the bank. Well, she called the police and said she was robbed."

"Did she know who did it?" Junior asked.

"She said she thought she was being followed, and then some guy hit her on the head from behind. He grabbed the money, and she looked up from the ground just in time to see him running away."

"So she didn't see his face?" Junior asked.

"That's right," Prissy said. "She didn't see his face at all. She did describe him a little bit, though. She said he was wearing a blue cardigan sweater."

"Did they find a suspect?" Junior asked.

"Yes. They found two suspects who were wearing blue cardigans!" Prissy said.

"That's quite a fashion statement about the neighborhood," Junior said. "How did they figure out which guy did it?" Junior asked.

"Well, that's the thing. The policeman decided the woman was lying because she wouldn't have been able to see the buttons on the front of the sweater to know it was a cardigan if she only saw him running away. That didn't make sense to me," Prissy said.

"Why not?" Junior said. "She said his back was turned because he was running away...." He stopped to imagine the scene. "Oh, I see what you mean!"

What was wrong with the policeman's conclusion?

Answer on page 91.

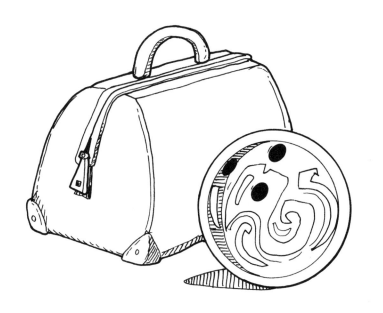

Terry Taggert's Terrible Day

Officer Longarm asked Dr. J. L. Quicksolve to help out when his friend Terry Taggert was arrested. Terry was a guard for an armored truck company.

"I just picked up a bag of money from the Tinsel Lanes Bowlorama," Terry explained. "I also picked up my wife's new bowling ball. Tina is a professional bowler. She always gets her bowling balls from Tinsel. He does good work. She ordered it, and since I was there anyway, I picked it up for her. It was a beauty. It was a bright, clear blue with white lines waving through it. Bowling balls these days remind me of the marbles I used when I was a kid. Anyway, when I got outside, this big guy walks up behind me and pokes a gun in my ribs. 'Stickup,' he whispers in my ear. I drop the moneybag and the bowling ball. He hits me on the head and knocks me out.

When I wake up, I'm all alone! No money! No bowling ball! Now they say I took the money! So where's the bowling ball, then? Let them tell me that! Better yet! Let them tell Tina! After losing her bowling ball, I think I'm safer here in jail until somebody straightens this out!"

Two days later, Officer Longarm came to see Dr. Quicksolve. "We found a suspect, but no money yet. Turk Sparkens, a known thief, lives just half a block from the bowling alley. He's a big guy and he rents an apartment from a fortune teller named Wanda," Officer Longarm said.

"Do you have any clues at all?" Dr. Quicksolve asked.

"Well, I went over there to talk to him, and Wanda wanted to tell my fortune. I said she could, thinking I might get a chance to look around a little for some reason to get a search warrant. Sure enough, the crystal ball turned out to be a bright blue bowling ball that looked to be brand new. So we got a search warrant, but we didn't find anything. There were no fingerprints on the ball except Wanda's. Turk claimed he bought it for her as a present to tell fortunes with. It looks like he did, so I'm afraid he's going to get away with the crime since we don't have any evidence," Officer Longarm said.

"Don't be so sure you don't have evidence," Dr. Quicksolve said.

What did Dr. Quicksolve mean about having evidence?

Answer on page 93.

Jump Rope

The school gym was crowded with jump ropers. They leaked out into the halls and onto the playground. Over 200 people, mostly kids from the school, were jumping rope for charity. They jumped in teams of six, with individuals taking turns jumping and going for as many hours as they could. Dr. J. L. Quicksolve stood out among his team members, being 40 years older and at least two feet taller than the kids on his team. He needed a longer rope. He did his share, though, putting in 15 to 20 minutes of rope jumping when it was his turn. He jumped rope at home frequently, so it was easy for him to maintain an even pace without getting too tired or out of breath.

When he finished his turn, he went out into the hall to get a drink of water. He was surprised to see Sergeant

Rebekah Shurshot talking to the principal. She saw him and came over to talk with him.

They exchanged greetings. Sergeant Shurshot made a friendly remark about Dr. Quicksolve's argyle socks and Bermuda shorts. He laughed good-naturedly and pointed to his tee shirt that had the word "Hope" printed across the front of it in bold blue letters. "It's for a good cause," he said.

Then Sergeant Shurshot explained why she was in the school. "There was a robbery late last night," she said. "Someone came in and robbed the custodian, Jake Duster, after everyone else had left the building. Jake said the robber must have sneaked in about two hours after everyone else had left. The guy came up behind Jake while he was vacuuming the office area. He forced Jake to unlock the principal's office. He took all the money they had collected for the Hope Jumpathon. Then he brought Jake out here into the hall and tied his hands. He took Jake's keys and locked the office doors. Then he locked Jake in the building when he went out the front door there."

Dr. Quicksolve looked at the row of doors to the main entrance to the school. "I know Jake Duster, and he's pretty smart. I'm surprised he thought you'd believe that story," Dr. Quicksolve said.

What did Dr. Quicksolve mean?

Answer on page 89.

Laughing Matters

Prissy Powers, the cutest girl on the cheerleading squad, stood on the edge of the diving board that extended out over the clear blue water of her Aunt Lucy's diamond-shaped swimming pool.

She inched back toward the edge until only her toes remained touching the board. She bent her knees, bounced once, and stretched her arms upward as she gracefully arced into the air, circled up perfectly and came straight down, knifing into the water, and causing barely a ripple to its glasslike surface. She swam to the side of the pool where Junior Quicksolve sat with his legs hanging into the water. He clapped his hands and laughed. "Great dive!" he said.

Prissy pulled herself out of the pool and sat beside her friend. She looked up at the clear blue sky. She squinted her eyes at the bright yellow sun. "Isn't it nice today?" she said.

Her Aunt Lucy was Lucy Looker, the beautiful and famous movie star, and she had asked Prissy and Junior to look after her house in Ann Arbor. They were welcome to use the swimming pool, and they were taking advantage of the opportunity. Prissy was allowed to have four friends over to swim. The others had not arrived yet, so they left the front door unlocked for them.

At one end of the pool, just on the grass and in the shade of two large lilac bushes, sat a large golden retriever. It was Junior's dog, Copper.

Junior looked at Copper and slid into the water. "Ahh!" he yelled. He thrashed around, splashing in the water as if he were drowning. Copper leaped into action. He jumped into the pool, creating a huge, noisy splash. He paddled to Junior who held onto Copper's neck to be pulled to the side of the pool. Copper climbed out having done his job, shook the water off his coat, and bounced back to his position in the shade. Prissy and Junior both laughed.

"You sure have him trained," Prissy said.

"I didn't really train him to do that," Junior replied. "He just seems to do it naturally." Then he said, "I'll get us a soda." He hopped up and turned toward the house where he saw two men. One of them was very short and very round. The other one was very tall and very thin. They would have looked very funny if it weren't for the ski masks and the revolvers they held pointed at the two young people.

Copper looked at the two men in masks and holding guns. He wasn't impressed. Despite what you might think, he wasn't a watchdog. The masks and guns meant nothing to him. As far as he was concerned, the two

intruders with masks and guns were welcome guests. He only wished they would "drown" so he could rescue them.

Junior and Prissy were directed into the house. The round burglar directed by pointing his gun. No one said a word.

When they were in the house, Junior could see the burglars had been there a while. Their loot was already in boxes and sitting near the front door.

"Tie them up and lock them in the garage," the skinny one said. Junior thought they must take turns being boss.

The round man took them into the attached three-car garage where Lucy's pickup truck and Jeep were parked. He made them sit down on the concrete floor where

Lucy usually parked her sports car. He made Prissy tie Junior's hands in front of him. He tied Prissy's hands together in front of her. Then he took a long rope and wrapped it around their waists, tying them together with their backs pressed against each other.

As they sat there on the floor, the tall masked man appeared and took a set of keys out of his pocket. Prissy recognized the keys as the ones Aunt Lucy had given her. She had left them on the kitchen counter. The man climbed into the truck and started the engine. Then he went to the door to the house and reached up above the button that operated the electric garage door opener. He yanked out the thin wire that snaked up the wall and across the ceiling.

"You won't last long," the tall one said to them in a husky voice that was obviously meant to sound menacing.

Then the two masked men went into the house and closed the door. Junior and Prissy could hear the click of the lock. They sat in the darkened garage listening to the humming of the truck engine. Prissy spoke first. "Do you have your pocket knife?" she said.

"Yes. I think we can untie ourselves without it, though," Junior said. "I almost laughed out loud at that guy!" he said.

Prissy laughed and said, "I know what you mean, but I'm glad you didn't!"

They both sat there, smiling in the dark a few more seconds. They stood up and began untying the ropes.

What did they think was so funny?

Answer on page 91.

Sergeant Shurshot
Solves a Case

"This homicide investigation isn't going too well," Lieutenant Rootumout said. He sat behind his desk and swung his legs up to rest his feet on the corner of it. He stretched back and folded his hands together. He was very relaxed for someone whose murder case wasn't going too well.

Maybe the reason for his nonchalance was his confidence in the people he was talking to. Sergeant Rebekah Shurshot sat directly in front of his desk. Officer Longarm and Officer Beekerjar, the police scientist, sat on either side of Sergeant Shurshot. Off to one side, as if he were merely an observer, sat the famous detective Dr. J. L. Quicksolve.

"Well, sir," Sergeant Shurshot said, "we have that green, bloodstained, fleece jogging outfit that was found along the road two miles from the scene of the crime."

"We've matched the blood of Susan Longded with the blood on the jogging outfit," Officer Beekerjar said. "It's definitely her blood, and it's most likely what the killer was wearing when he bludgeoned her to death."

"We have pictures of Malisha Demone, the victim's business partner, wearing a jogging outfit just like the one we found," Officer Longarm said. "We searched her house, and didn't find a jogging outfit there like the one in the picture. She said she never had a green outfit like that. She claimed the coloring in the picture wasn't right."

Sergeant Shurshot said, "All we found were those two cats—a black one and a white one—and a very nervous canary."

"I went to the nearest pet shop," Officer Longarm said. "The manager knew Malisha Demone very well. He said she was quite a bird lover. He said she buys another canary nearly every week! She said she bought them for her cousins, nephews, and nieces."

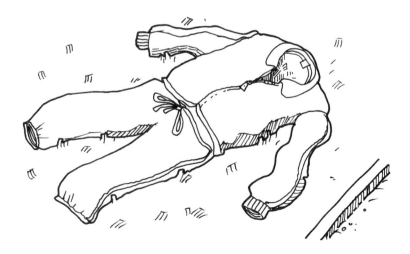

Sergeant Shurshot said, "I went back to ask her about all the birds. The one that was there before was gone. Malisha said one of her cats got it when she accidentally left the cage door open. All I got from that trip was cat hair all over my uniform." Officer Longarm said, "I think she's getting those birds for the cats to eat! I think she just likes to watch the chase!"

"And the kill," Sergeant Shurshot added.

"If we could just prove the bloodstained outfit belonged to Malisha, we would have a case," Officer Longarm said. "We know they fought with each other at work a lot."

"Wait," Sergeant Shurshot said, sitting up in her chair. She looked at Officer Beekerjar. "I think we can do that!"

Officer Beekerjar looked puzzled as he thought that over for a minute. Then he said, "I see what you mean."

How can they prove Malisha owned the outfit?

Answer on page 91.

The Bike in the Bushes

When Bulow Pepperstein and his wife, Claudia, retired, they chose to buy a nice little three-bedroom ranch house in Dr. J. L. Quicksolve's subdivision that laced out into the countryside, bordered by farms and fields. Some would call it urban sprawl; others would just call it a nice place to live. The house they bought backed up to Crane Road, a through street that marked one edge of the subdivision. It had little traffic, and the pavement on Crane Road ended at the corner of the subdivision, where it continued into the farmland as a gravel road. The Peppersteins planted a row of lilac bushes to serve as a privacy wall between their house and the road. The bushes hadn't grown very much. They were actually little more than three feet tall. So Crane Road and all that went on there could be seen quite easily by Junior and his friend Skeeter as they marched back and forth pushing lawn mowers, cutting the grass as a

kind of welcome to the neighborhood for the Peppersteins.

The boys stopped to rest from their work under the
hot summer sun. They met at the corner of the house,
where they had placed a pitcher of lemonade in the
shade.

Suddenly, a silver Honda minivan came racing up the
road. It jolted to a halt as it pulled to the side of the
road. The boys watched with interest while a young
brown-haired man hopped out of the driver's seat,

looked around suspiciously, and opened the back door of the van.

Junior and Skeeter couldn't believe it when they saw the man pull an expensive-looking mountain bike out of the van, wheel it over to the side, and toss it into the bushes.

The man, who had some kind of red scarf around his neck, jumped back into the van and roared away, leaving the bicycle lying there in the bushes. The boys ran over to the bicycle.

"Nice bike," Junior said.

"Why do you think he left it here?" Skeeter asked, then answered with the following:

"Maybe there was someone else in the van—like his son or something. They were arguing, and the dad got angry, so he threw the kid's new bike out, figuring the kid would learn a lesson if he had to walk back and get it."

"That might be it, but it sounds a little far-fetched to me," Junior said. "Let's go into the house and call my dad. We can find out what he thinks," Junior said.

The boys walked back to the Peppersteins', where they took off their shoes and dusted the grass off their pants before they went inside to call Dr. Quicksolve.

Skeeter listened while Junior told his dad what they had seen. Suddenly Junior said, "Okay," and slammed down the phone. "Let's go!" he yelled. The boys ran out of the house and back to the edge of the road.

"It's gone!" Skeeter said.

"Man!" Junior said. "I bet my dad was right!"

What did Dr. Quicksolve think was going on?

Answer on page 90.

Miss Match

Miss Match was Junior's favorite teacher in middle school. Her name, unquestionably, described her wardrobe. She mixed stripes and checks and plaids and polka dots in a cornucopia of colors haphazardly splattered across a painter's palette. Yet for Miss Match and her bubbling personality, it worked. She was Junior's teacher in English, social studies, and world history.

Mismatched is how you felt when you went up against her on an intellectual level concerning nearly any subject. If a student was not in class to learn on any given class day, he quite likely would find himself back at school on a Saturday morning until Miss Match decided he had achieved a certain level of enthusiasm for learning.

To Miss Match, all the world and life itself was a mystery to be solved, and recalcitrance in a student was a bull to be wrestled to the ground. People were not meant to go stumbling through life like a drunk in the dark. No, people needed to build a base of knowledge to stand on and to illuminate the darkness ahead. Start with facts, learned through repetition, questions and answers, clear thinking, and more practice, practice, practice. Miss Match stood ready to face the challenge of providing exactly the illumination young minds needed to move forward in this world, whether it was how to introduce your date to your parents on prom night or knowing why Caesar crossed the Rubicon.

Jocko

Miss Match struck a pose in her Madras shirt and polka-dot skirt. She had added a three-cornered hat, pretending she was George Washington crossing the Delaware. Her antics ignited a burst of laughter from Junior Quicksolve's history class. Miss Match was like that. She brought history alive with her imagination and enthusiasm and kept the attention of the students with her unusual outfit combinations and her animated personality.

Junior liked to sit along the wall to the teacher's right near the middle of the classroom. He could sit sideways in his chair a little and see the teacher and the whole class, not to mention Prissy Powers, his close friend and the cutest girl on the cheerleading squad, who sat next to him. He laughed along with the rest of the class, but then they all settled down when Miss Match began to speak.

"There is one person who helped General Washington during the American Revolutionary War and was also famous during the Civil War," she said.

Skeeter raised his hand and said, "How can that be? There were nearly a hundred years between those two wars!"

"That is a good point, Skeeter," Miss Match said. "He actually died during the Revolutionary War serving his country and General Washington. He was a young boy who held the general's horse when he went into battle. That is how the story goes. He was called Jocko, and he

became famous for a while for his steadfast courage and loyalty. George Washington had a statue made in honor of Jocko. Many others made copies of this little statue to put in their yards. The tradition continues today."

"But what did he do in the Civil War if he was killed in the Revolutionary War?" Skeeter persisted.

"That's another good question," Miss Match said. "Let me give you a clue. It was in our reading last week, and it was about the Underground Railroad. Remember? The Underground Railroad was a network of people and homes that stretched from the South across the North, clear to Canada. They were people who helped slaves escape to freedom. Now who knows what part these little statues played in the Underground Railroad?"

Junior started to raise his hand, but Prissy's hand shot up first. "I know!" she said excitedly.

Do you know?

Answer on page 92.

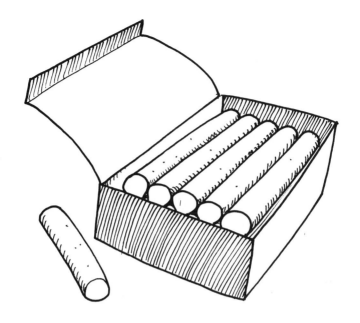

Chalk Snake

Students never really knew what Miss Match would do next. Most did not want to test her, but there were a few—like the student who knew Miss Match always used the chalkboard when she was teaching. She often explained that we learn best when we listen with our ears and see with our eyes, and when we say things out loud. Also, when we write things down on paper, they go right up our arms to our brains. Of course, the more times we see, hear, say, and write things down, the better we learn them. So she would tell students to write down their spelling words, history lessons, etc., and tape the lessons above the sink so they could practice saying them out loud while they helped in the kitchen. So it was important for her to write things on the chalkboard when she was teaching her class a lesson—outlining the main ideas and teaching her students to take notes as she spoke.

Of course, she wouldn't have pieces of chalk lying around her immaculately organized classroom, tempting students to write on the board between classes. The chalk was always neatly put away in a box in a certain corner of a certain desk drawer. And everyone knew it.

One day in Junior's history class, Miss Match was explaining how the Scottish kilt was modeled after the attire of the Roman soldiers who formed a phalanx, a virtual wall, with their overlapping shields. She opened her drawer to get a piece of chalk from the box. Though the room was always quiet when Miss Match was speaking, that quiet seemed to have an unusual, almost eerie thickness to it as Miss Match opened the chalk box while she spoke and glanced down at the coiled garter snake that one of Junior's less discerning classmates had put there.

Miss Match...

Did what?

Answer on page 89.

No Germs Allowed

Miss Match stood strong and thin—robust, as she walked down the rows of desks and lectured to Junior's history class. She wore a long gray dress and red socks and black high-top tennis shoes. Her lectures often consisted of story after story. Junior enjoyed her stories, and he didn't mind that occasionally he heard the same story in history class that he had just heard the hour before in English class.

Miss Match was talking about her Spartan upbringing in the "Copper Country" of Michigan's Upper Peninsula. She spoke of the real Spartans, the warrior people of the ancient Greek city-state called Sparta. Children were brought up to be strong and aggressive warriors. Very young boys would often be taken away from home to be trained as soldiers. Part of the training was that they had to depend on their own wiles even to

eat. They had to steal food or starve. They weren't
punished for stealing, but they were punished for being
caught!

Miss Match described Spartan women—wives and
mothers—waiting for the soldiers to return from battle.
The greatest shame was to retreat. If a man died in battle,
the first question would be about where he was
wounded—whether his "hurts were in front or behind."
If his wounds were on his back as if he had fled the
battlefield, he was a terrible disgrace to his family.

Miss Match announced that everyone had done a good
job on the homework. "I'm still taking Skeeter's work to
him at home," Junior said when Miss Match handed
Junior's papers to him.

"Oh, yes," Miss Match said. "I have his homework on

my desk." She turned and took a large, brown envelope from her desk. "Here it is. Skeeter did well. His next assignment is in there, too."

The bell rang. Junior picked up his things and headed to the door, where he was met by his friend Prissy Powers.

"What's that?" Prissy asked, indicating the brown envelope Junior had tucked under his arm.

"It's Skeeter's homework," Junior answered. He absent-mindedly opened the envelope and slid out the papers that were inside. "He should be back at school soon."

The papers made a crackling sound in Junior's hand.

"What's that?" Prissy asked, reaching to touch the stiff paper that was Skeeter's homework.

"Ha!" Junior laughed. "Leave it to Miss Match to kill the germs!"

What had Miss Match done to Skeeter's home-work papers?

Answer on page 92.

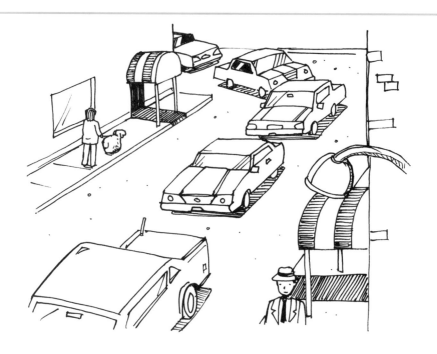

Jekyll Tries to Hide

In spite of terrorist threats, Ambassador Treaty insisted on arriving precisely as scheduled. He would arrive at the embassy at 10:30 A.M. to give his televised speech. So, a little before then, five unmarked police cars were winding their way through town. Ambassador Treaty was in the middle car with his bodyguards. Dr. J. L. Quicksolve, Sergeant Rebekah Shurshot, Officer Alvin Boysenberry, and Detective Elliott Savant were in the lead car.

"The problem is Jekyll," Sergeant Shurshot said rather nervously.

"He's been under surveillance for a week," Boysenberry said as he drove the car slowly through the back streets of town.

"But he has that townhouse, just around the corner and only two blocks away," Sergeant Shurshot said.

"He can't shoot around corners," Boysenberry said.

"Everyone is expecting the ambassador at 10:30," Dr. Quicksolve said. "If we could just delay him a few minutes..."

"What about television?" Boysenberry said. "He's supposed to be on TV at 10:30."

"Stop!" Elliott suddenly shouted.

Boysenberry slammed the car to a halt. They heard the screech of tires as the cars behind reacted to the surprise.

"What's...?"

Not waiting for Boysenberry to finish his question, Elliott shouted, "Release the hood!" Elliott jumped out of the car, and immediately the ambassador's car was surrounded by policemen with guns in their hands.

Elliott stood in front of the car staring down at the engine, which purred like a kitten. His black curly hair was blowing hysterically in the wind. He peeked around the raised car hood.

Dr. Quicksolve got out of the car, smiling at Elliott and shaking his head. He spoke quietly to Elliott. "Not very discreet, Elliott," he whispered.

Lieutenant Rootumout ran up to them. "What's going on?" he demanded.

"I thought I should check the wiper fluid," Elliott said casually. He bent down under the hood, reached in for a minute, and said, "It's okay."

"That was a good idea," Dr. Quicksolve said, supporting Elliott and confounding Lieutenant Rootumout. Unwilling to question Dr. Quicksolve's judgment, he stood there stammering. Officer Boysenberry ran up to

them and voiced the lieutenant's great frustration.

"We're going to be really late!" Boysenberry said excitedly. "What are the TV stations going to do?" he asked, shouting.

"Commercials," Dr. Quicksolve said calmly.

Another officer in uniform came running up to them. "There's been an explosion on the podium!" he said. "We've gotten orders to take Ambassador Treaty to a safe place. The speech has been canceled."

An unmarked van was parked across the street from the townhouse where the suspected terrorist known as Jekyll was staying. It was much too crowded for comfort. Detective Elliott Savant squatted in the back of the van in the middle of various kinds of electronic equipment. The two policemen who had been stationed in the van when the bombing occurred were explaining what Jekyll was doing at the time.

"Jekyll wasn't involved, at least as far as we could tell," said Murphy, the redheaded officer who sat in the driver's seat. Shea, Officer Murphy's partner, spoke up from the other front seat. "He was pulling out of his driveway. He was sitting right there in his car when we heard the explosion. Then we saw him drive off in the other direction."

"Did you see anything that looked suspicious?" Dr. Quicksolve asked.

"We've been watching this place for two days," Murphy said. "We haven't seen anything unusual...nothing today except a paperboy." He looked down at his clipboard. "Yesterday we watched people come and go from their townhouses. There was a mailman who was here yesterday. The phone company had guys working up in

those trees along the street for a couple hours. A couple of people walked by and two girls on bicycles rode by. That was it."

"He's gone now. Maybe we could get out of the van for a minute," Lieutenant Rootumout suggested.

"Good idea," Dr. Quicksolve said. "Maybe we can find something."

As they began to climb out, they noticed the back door of the van had already been opened. "Oh, no!" Boysenberry said. Elliott was gone.

Dr. Quicksolve, Sergeant Shurshot, and Lieutenant Rootumout walked across the street and looked at the front of the townhouse. The building stretched the length of the block. It was simply a series of front doors and garage doors that sat close to the street. It was a quiet tree-lined street, and there was little to see.

Boysenberry, whose job was basically to keep an eye on Detective Elliott Savant, ran back and forth on the sidewalk in front of the building like a hound trying to pick up a scent. Then he ran for the corner as if he had gotten a whiff of something.

"He could have used radio control to set off the bomb," Sergeant Shurshot suggested.

"Good thought," Dr. Quicksolve said.

Lieutenant Rootumout looked down the street where Officer Boysenberry stood near the corner flapping his arms in exasperation. "You can't go through this building or around that corner with radio control," Lieutenant Rootumout said.

"Oh?" Dr. Quicksolve said. Then he shouted to Boysenberry. "Look up!"

"What?" Boysenberry said.

"Look up! In the tree!"

Boysenberry looked up into the tree he was standing under. Then he looked back toward Dr. Quicksolve and threw his arms up, showing his confusion.

"Try the next one!" Dr. Quicksolve said.

Boysenberry took a couple steps back toward his friends and looked up into the next tree. Suddenly a head plopped down in front of him. Elliott hung there upside down from a tree limb with a big upside down smile. He handed something to Boysenberry.

"There!" Dr. Quicksolve said.

What was going on?

Answer on page 93.

Panic for Donuts

If you knew cars and you knew Elliott Savant, you wouldn't be surprised to learn that he drove a reconditioned, bright red 1949 Pontiac Chieftain convertible. To many people, its somewhat bloated and rounded lines made it look like it was made of bread dough. Such were the aerodynamics of 1949.

Elliott was a very close friend of Dr. J. L. Quicksolve and his family. Some people said the two of them looked like brothers. Elliott often took Dr. Quicksolve's son, Junior, and Junior's twin cousins, Flora and Fauna, on daylong excursions in the convertible.

The girls were excited as they climbed into the backseat of Elliott's car. They loved riding with the top down. They were delirious when they asked Elliott where they were going and he said, "We're going to Panic for

donuts." They screamed in mock terror, and they all four laughed uncontrollably for several minutes every time the word "Panic" came up. Elliott's explanation that Panic was a small town about 70 miles away did little to change their reaction each time Elliott said, "Panic."

"What's wrong?" Elliott would say, once the laughter died down.

"Where are we going?" Flora would ask.

"To Panic!" Elliott would answer. The girls would scream directly into each other's face. Then they would laugh and laugh.

By the time Elliott caught on, they were close enough to the small town that signs began to appear as they got ever closer.

Approaching Panic, one sign read.

Screams!

Nearing Panic, another sign read.

Screams!

Finally, Entering Panic.

This time Elliott joined in the screams, and Junior did actually panic, afraid they would all be arrested for disturbing the peace. He insisted Elliott stop the car so they could all compose themselves.

They sat on the edge of town quietly composing themselves. Elliott led everyone in deep breathing exercises. Along the side of the road, in front of them, was a sign that said, "Panic—Population 95, 94, 93." Each number was crossed out and a lower number replaced it. By this time the girls were too exhausted to react, but Junior looked at the declining numbers and said, "Must be the killer donuts!"

"The donuts are great!" Elliott said, not getting

Junior's joke. "They're worth the trip, even with the noise."

"You love it!" Flora said.

"The noise!" Fauna said.

They sat there quietly for a few more minutes.

Elliott spoke first. "I was just thinking," he said.

"What?" Junior said.

"I was thinking about riding a horse."

Junior and the twins looked around. There were no horses.

"Oh?" Junior said.

"Yes," Elliott said. "What if you were riding along thinking so hard that..."

"I never try to think that hard," Flora said.

"Believe it," Fauna said.

Elliott continued. "What if your saddle slipped around the horse while he was trotting along, and you went with it? You would be upside down on a horse, in quite a pickle. I think it's good to think about things so you don't—" he caught himself before saying that particular word— "get too upset. What would you do?"

Junior looked back at the girls who were twisting their necks and trying to put their heads down into a position so they could imagine the predicament Elliott had described.

"I don't think you would want to drop on your head. And if you did, you would quite likely scare the horse and get kicked or trampled," Junior said.

"I would say, 'Whoa!'" Flora said.

"Then you would just be hanging there upside down, holding on for dear life," Junior said.

"We're getting hungry! We give up!" the twins said in unison.

What did Elliott say about the horse problem?

Answer on page 91.

Guards

Detective Elliott Savant was quite a sight as he rode his mule, Mollie, out into the pasture. He wore his wide-brimmed sombrero and made "chuck! chuck!" sounds as he patiently guided his mule to the left and right, herding the dozen goats toward one corner of the fenced area. At the other corner stood two donkeys, contentedly doing nothing.

The little animal enthusiastically trotting back and forth behind Mollie didn't look like a sheepdog. It was definitely not a sheepdog. It was Elliott's bulldog, Marguerite, playing her role as a goat herder. Junior thought Marguerite should be wearing a sombrero like Elliott's.

Elliott pulled on the reins, turning Mollie, and they began to pick up speed as Mollie trotted toward him. Without Mollie slowing at all, Junior was suddenly and smoothly scooped up onto the running mule's back, right behind Elliott.

They trotted back to the barn. Junior's friend Skeeter sat on the fence cheering. "Wow!" Skeeter said. "That was great!"

"Do you want to try it?" Elliott asked Skeeter.

"Not today," Skeeter said nervously.

They'd been invited to the ranch of Sam and Barb Brawler. The Brawlers had moved to this Texas ranch when it was all woods and brush. After clearing out the brush, they had explained earlier that day, they had found a set of stones placed in a circle. They dug beneath the stones, and water began gushing out rapidly. "We researched this property and found this was a well that served a small town that used to be right here," Sam explained, taking off his cowboy hat and wiping his forehead with his red bandana.

Sam directed them to a small brick building, which he unlocked, and they all went inside. "This is what we finally were able to make out of what turned out to be an artesian well," he said. "We got the rights to set in a pipe that extends three miles away from here. We provide pure well water for three bottled water companies."

"Some people strike oil, and some people strike water!" Junior said.

They walked out of the building and looked across the beautiful ranch at the large house, the pond, and the big yard that apparently was also a pasture for the goats and the two donkeys.

"We have goats to cut the grass for us," Barb said.

"Why do you have the donkey?" Skeeter asked.

"Coyotes," Barb said.

"Coyotes?" Skeeter asked, puzzled by the answer.

"Donkeys scare away the coyotes, don't they?" Junior said.

"That was the idea," Barb said, "but all these guys do is stay to themselves on the other side of the yard. We don't know what to do."

"There might be a way to solve your problem," Elliott said. "Do you know someone who wants to buy a donkey?"

"How about two donkeys?" Barb said.

"No," Elliott said.

What was Elliott's solution?

Answer on page 94.

Stealing Bases/Stealing Cars

S mack! The sound of the softball hitting the catcher's mitt was like the crack of a rifle shot. Junior Quicksolve stood along the fence on the third base line next to the dugout of the Ann Arbor Area Police softball team, the Lawmen. Junior checked the readout on the radar gun he held to check the speed of Elliott Savant's pitches...94 mph! Elliott had pitched a no-hitter so far. Now, with one strike on the batter, he was just two good pitches away from a one–zero shutout, thanks to a home run by his teammate, Officer Longarm.

The most nervous person on the field was not the pitcher or the coach, Dr. Quicksolve, who stood ramrod straight in the center of the dugout blowing a large, pink bubble with his chewing gum. No, the nervous one, pacing back and forth in the dirt in front of the dugout and wearing a shirt strapped across her back with a big zero on it, was Detective Elliott Savant's bulldog, Marguerite. She paused with each pitch and watched the batter intently until she heard the ball smack into the catcher's mitt.

The lights came on as it began to get dark. In spite of the fact that the game had been quite a pitcher's duel, it had been a long one. There was a delay early in the game caused by a large patch of dark clouds that produced thunder and lightning, but no ran fell in the immediate area.

Now the batter, the other team's first baseman, was standing on the first base side of the plate ready for the pitch. He wore a large number sixteen on his back. Number six, the other team's shortstop, stood on third base. When he had batted, he had just made enough contact with the ball to keep it in fair territory, hitting to the opposite field, down the first base line. The right fielder had missed the ball. It bounced off his glove, and the batter advanced to third with a triple on the error.

Elliott's pitching arm came blasting around with blinding speed. The ball shot to the catcher like a bullet. Compounding the batter's dilemma was the fact that Elliott wore no glove, so he could pitch with either hand. The batter did not know until the last instant which side of the pitcher the ball would be coming from. The batter had little time to focus on the speeding ball. Strike two!

Again, Elliott paused at the mound, facing the batter. He stepped forward, and this time it was his left arm that whirled the ball forward at blinding speed. The batter

squared around to bunt and just held his bat out in the middle of the strike zone. The runner on third came charging down the line as the left-handed batter sent the ball out five feet in front of the plate, where it landed, spinning in the dirt. It was a perfect bunt.

The catcher tried to step forward to get the ball, but the incoming base runner's slide to the plate forced him to leap in the air to avoid the collision. He still managed to stay on his feet, and he reached for the spinning ball and threw to first base just ahead of the runner. The run counted, making it a tie game.

Suddenly the clouds in the dark sky seemed to break loose, and there was a deluge of rain that sent everyone running to their cars.

Dr. Quicksolve sat behind the steering wheel of his yellow VW Beetle, and Elliott sat beside him. They watched the rain pour down so hard, they couldn't even see the ballfield. Junior sat in the back seat, drying Marguerite with a towel.

"It looks like we won't be able to finish the game," Elliott said. "It will end in a tie."

"People are leaving," Junior said, watching the lights of several cars moving out of the parking lot toward the exit. "But at least we have the donuts!" he said. He held up a white bag of donuts and a thermos of hot chocolate.

They sat there for almost half an hour before the rain slowed to a sprinkle and finally stopped. Water still dripped from the trees. Dr. Quicksolve got out of the car to talk to the other coach and the umpire.

When he came back to the car, he opened the door and

sat down. "It's over," he said. "Too many players have left."

Suddenly, a car came racing into the parking lot. It skidded to a stop next to them, and Officer Longarm jumped out and ran over to them. When Dr. Quicksolve rolled his window down, Officer Longarm said, "I was carjacked! It was one of the other players. He wore a bandana over his face, so I'm not sure which one he was. He had a gun, and he forced me to drive. I couldn't reach his gun hand, but I managed to grab his other hand when we were about four blocks from here. Then when he brought the gun around, I grabbed for it. I think he sprained my arm. It might even be broken. He jumped out of the car and ran off. I could see a '6' on the back of his jersey. He must have been number six or sixteen. I don't think they had another player with a six on his jersey. I couldn't tell which one it was, though."

"At least we know who probably did it," Elliott said.

Dr. Quicksolve nodded in agreement, and Officer Longarm stood there with a puzzled look on his face.

How did Elliott know who did it?

Answer on page 93.

Portage Lake Burglar

Detective Elliott Savant stopped rowing the little wooden rowboat when he had gotten about 40 feet out from the shore where Sergeant Rebekah Shurshot and Officer Boysenberry were discussing the latest burglary in a string of five break-ins at cottages on Portage Lake. Two county sheriff's deputies were crouched down toward the ground watching Officer Beekerjar carefully pulling up a plaster cast of a footprint in the sand.

Suddenly, a short, round, muscled bulldog loped out from the side of the cottage and ran the length of the dock that stretched 15 feet out from the shore. She tumbled into the water like a sack of potatoes with stubby little legs. The splash nearly reached shore.

"There goes Marguerite," Sergeant Shurshot said, referring to Elliott's bulldog, who had surfaced and was now paddling her way out to Elliott's boat.

"She'll be all right," Elliott said as if Sergeant Shurshot could hear him from that distance. In fact, she could hear him because they both wore hands-free cell phones clipped to their ears.

The other officers could hear him too. "Why are you out there?" Boysenberry asked nervously.

"I wanted to get a view of the cottages from out here," Elliott answered. He stood in the little boat throwing one arm out as if he were casting an imaginary fishing line. Then he started wheeling his other hand around as if he had hooked a..."dogfish," he whispered. He continued reeling.

"Did Beekerjar get a good cast of that shoeprint?" Elliott asked. Marguerite finally reached the boat, and Elliott bent down and hoisted the dripping bulldog into the little dinghy. She immediately shook herself enough to sufficiently soak her master. Then she sat down on the wooden seat of the boat as if to say, "I'm captain now."

"It is a pretty good print," Beekerjar said. "But I don't think it'll be enough to pin this on our suspect, Slick Slimer. It looks like an ordinary leather-soled shoe. The sand didn't pick up any distinguishing marks. I could probably figure out a shoe size, though."

Elliott sat down and began rowing back toward shore. "Get a search warrant. I want to visit Slick's cottage."

When they arrived at the small white cottage on the other side of the lake, a blue convertible was in the driveway. When Sergeant Shurshot knocked on the door, there was no answer. "That's his car," she said.

"Check around in back by the lake," Elliott told Boysenberry, who immediately walked around the cottage to see what he could find.

Boysenberry came back around the corner. "Slick and his girlfriend are sitting out on the beach," he said. "They didn't see me."

The police officers started to walk around toward the beach. Elliott pulled a small knife from his pocket, flicked it open, and tried the door, which opened easily. "Go ahead," he said and entered the cottage.

When Slick saw the police officers, he jumped up, stubbing his bare toes against his lounge chair, and shouted angrily, "Haven't you bothered me enough? I told you all I know about those burglaries. I got a record, so you keep bugging me about this stuff! I told you I'm not your man! You better have a search warrant this time!"

"We do," Sergeant Shurshot said. "We're going to...."

Just then, Elliott stepped out of the back door of the cottage. He walked toward them and said, "Let's go. Nothing here."

Sergeant Shurshot looked frustrated at the sudden suggestion that they leave, but she trusted Elliott enough to turn and follow him toward the police cars. She could not help asking quietly, "What's up?"

"We will get him next time," Elliott said confidently.

What did Elliott do to give him this confidence?

Answer on page 90.

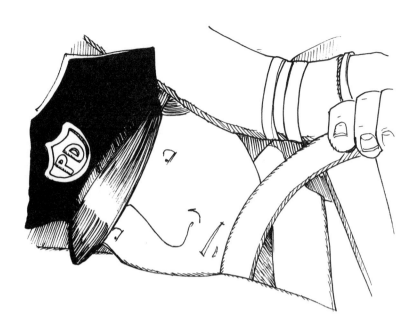

Across a Crowded Room

Their heads were so close their ears touched, and their chins rested on the dashboard. "How else could we get 10 people in a police car?" Officer Alvin Boysenberry whispered to the other head, which belonged to Detective Elliott Savant. Boysenberry's left hand barely reached the top of the steering wheel. The weight of the two men on top of him crushed his shoulders down to the side of the steering wheel and forced his chin down firmly on the dashboard. His eyes were just high enough over the dashboard for him to see the street ahead. He drove slowly. The car wandered left and right, but Boysenberry somehow managed to keep it in the proper lane.

"But why do we have 10 people in our car, Boysenberry?" Elliott whispered. They were whispering

to be discreet, but the radio blared loudly from the speaker just in front of their noses, and the eight rookie officers wouldn't have heard them talking anyway.

"It's a federal program," Boysenberry said. He paused as if that were enough to explain anything. Then he continued, "When the department accepted federal money to hire two extra officers, there were contingencies. Bringing along these rookie officers for a field observation was part of it. I thought they asked you about it."

"They asked if we could bring some rookie officers along, yes. I didn't think they meant eight at a time!" Elliott said, not bothering to whisper anymore.

They pulled into the driveway of a small bungalow. They slowly piled out of the car and into the house. It took almost ten minutes to get everyone into the house. Elliott, Boysenberry, the eight rookie officers, Sergeant Rebekah Shurshot, Martha (the wife of the poisoned victim), Roger (her neighbor), and Bobby, a pizza boy who was waiting to be paid and became trapped in the house when the entourage of law officers arrived, all stood so close together, no one could move. They stood face to face and back to back, snaking around the furniture and down the halls of the house like a conga line of dancers who were at a loss as to what to do now that their music had stopped.

Sergeant Shurshot, Roger (the neighbor), and Martha (the wife) were each pressed in a different corner of the living room. Elliott and Boysenberry were pressed into the middle of the room with their backs locked together. Normal conversation was clearly impossible.

Sergeant Shurshot decided she could not discreetly report to Detective Savant any other way in this situation except to hand her notebook to the rookie officer whose back was pressed tightly against hers. She indicated that he was to pass the notebook to Elliott. Since Sergeant Shurshot communicated with gestures, waving the small notebook toward Elliott, the rookie officer did the same to the officer in front of him, who did the same to the officer in front of him, etc., until the notebook reached Detective Elliott Savant.

Elliott opened the notebook and read what Sergeant Shurshot had written so far. In her notebook, Sergeant Shurshot explained that Martha said she came home from bingo and found her husband dead on the living room floor. Elliott panicked for a second, looking up wide-eyed in shock. Then he looked back and read that the body had been removed. He was much relieved and pushed out of his mind the image of this crowd of people trampling the body of the deceased. Elliott continued his reading. Sergeant Shurshot wrote that she had just received a call on her cell phone that Frank Peterson had been poisoned. Clipped to the page was a note that was found on the kitchen table. It said, "Frank, I will be home too late for supper. There is chili in the refrigerator." The sergeant's report indicated the note was on the table next to a bowl of chili, a knife and fork, and a box of crackers.

Elliott, looking over the top of the head of the rookie officer directly in front of him, caught Roger's eye, and said, "What do you know about this, Roger?"

Because of the noise that filled the room, which was growing increasingly warm and stuffy, it was apparent to the rookie officer, whose ear Elliott had spoken directly into, that Roger couldn't hear Elliott's question. So he repeated it to the next rookie officer, etc., until the message finally got to Roger, who answered into the ear of the rookie officer who stood in front of him. The message got back to Elliott— "I knew Martha's chili was a killer! I warned Frank about that. Of course, I was talking about the heartburn."

As the message slowly worked its way around the room, everyone turned and stared suspiciously at Roger.

Elliott rotated his body like a penguin in a starched suit, until he faced Martha Peterson, who was standing in another corner of the room. He spoke into the nearest ear. "What can you tell me?" he asked.

The message worked its way to Martha Peterson, and her message came back, "I can't believe Frank is dead! I'm going to sue the company that made that box of crackers!"

"Why the knife and fork?" was Elliott's next question.

Martha's answer came back, "I make thick chili."

Elliott thought for a minute and said, "You're under arrest."

The frightened rookie officer in front of him raised both of his hands in the air and repeated the message. The whole process looked something like the "wave" at a baseball stadium until finally Martha Peterson raised her hands and fainted. She did not fall, though, simply because she did not have enough room.

Why did Elliott arrest the rookie officers?

Answer on page 93.

The General's Last Stop

General Robello pulled some political strings, invisible strings it seemed, to get his private bulletproof train car attached to a passenger train that would carry him on a tour across the United States. His plan was to see the United States and much of Canada, and avoid being assassinated. Back home in his tiny island nation, three attempts on his life had been made in as many months. As it turned out, he didn't accomplish either goal.

The train was stopped in Ann Arbor. The train, the station, and even the parking lot were surrounded by yellow police tape. Police officers swarmed around the area. Dr. Quicksolve, Sergeant Shurshot, and Lieutenant Rootumout stared into the open train car at the pajama-clad body of the general. The bunny slippers on his feet

pointed straight up in the air. The general was not embarrassed. His countrymen would be when the photographs appeared in the newspapers.

Officer Alvin Boysenberry was jogging down the center of Fuller Road, looking frantically back and forth. He had lost sight of Detective Elliott Savant again. That was important to Boysenberry. Keeping Detective Elliott Savant from getting truly lost while he was lost in thought was Boysenberry's primary job. The officer stopped and let out a sigh when he saw the familiar figure come out of Carlie's Bar and Grill wearing his trench coat and galoshes. His wild, curly, black hair and his black mustache left no doubt that this was the wayward detective.

Elliott was eating something out of a white paper bag he held in one hand. He marched past Boysenberry toward the train station.

"Onion rings," Elliott said as he passed Boysenberry.

The information was collected. There were two others in the private car besides the deceased. The general's aide, Captain Carou, had gone Western since his arrival in America, from his ten-gallon cowboy hat down to his fancy black and red cowboy boots. The other person was the general's large, round bodyguard, Sergeant Wade. Wade was resplendent in his paratrooper's uniform with a thick gold braid around one shoulder. His magnificent black combat boots gleamed brightly, and his bright red beret was tilted down toward one eye.

They both said they were at opposite ends of the long train car and unable to see each other or the general when the train car suddenly filled with smoke and some kind of gas that rendered them immediately unconscious. A gas mask was found behind a chair near the body of the general, who apparently had been strangled with a thin cord of some kind. No such cord was found lying around in the train car.

"I've heard of a case like this before," Sergeant Shurshot said, huddling for a brief conference with Dr. Quicksolve and Elliott Savant. "The likely scenario is that the sergeant set off the bomb, took off a shoelace from his combat boots, and strangled the general. He just relaced his boots to hide the murder weapon. He then pretended to be unconscious himself."

"I don't think we can pin it on the sergeant that easily at all," Elliott said.

Why not?

Answer on page 92.

If He Were Smart...

The Ann Arbor train station sat practically in the shadow of the towering University Hospital complex that dominated the horizon on the north side of town along the Huron River. So it was only a matter of minutes after the murder on the train was discovered before the two once trusted men, now suspects, were whisked away by ambulance to the hospital. Two policemen sat in each ambulance, guarding the only two people who really knew who killed General Robello.

Two trusted men, and one was the killer. They had been closed up together in the luxury train car of General Robello. One of them had set off a smoke bomb, a gas that caused the others to become unconscious while he did his deadly work of strangling the general to death. Sergeant Wade, the handsome muscular bodyguard, was certainly suspect. The shoelaces of his combat boots could have been the murder weapon.

What about the noble Captain Carou, decked out in his fancy cowboy boots? He was there and just as capable of committing the crime. The irony, of course, was that both of these men knew who was guilty and who was innocent.

"We need to talk to them," Dr. Quicksolve said as he climbed into his yellow VW Beetle. Sergeant Shurshot climbed into the passenger seat, and they sped toward the hospital.

"Let's go!" Officer Boysenberry said. He jumped behind the wheel of his black and white squad car. Detective Elliott Savant climbed into the front passenger seat. He reached down and pulled up an ornate plumed crash helmet that looked like a knight's helmet from the days of kings and castles. Boysenberry automatically pushed the button that opened the moon roof that allowed the colorful feathers on the top of the helmet to stick up above the roofline of the specially equipped police car.

Officer Beekerjar got into the backseat, and away they went...in the opposite direction of the hospital. Detective Savant and Officer Beekerjar were too deep in thought, each in his own little world, to notice that Boysenberry was so excited about being able to use his siren and flashing lights to race through town that he didn't really care what direction they were going. The conversations in the two separate cars were eerily similar.

Sergeant Shurshot said, "The lab reports from the scene may tell us something about who is the most likely suspect."

"That is right," Dr. Quicksolve said.

Officer Beekerjar said, "There may be fingerprints on the gas mask or residue on the person who ignited the gas bomb."

"Umm," said Elliott.

"There is motive to consider," Sergeant Shurshot said.

"That's true," Dr. Quicksolve said, "but either of the men might have been paid to kill the general."

"Which one would want to kill the general?" Boysenberry said. He had made several turns and was now driving past the railroad station for the second time. No one responded to his question.

Dr. Quicksolve stopped his VW in front of the hospital and reached for the ignition key to turn off the engine. "If he were smart," Dr. Quicksolve said, "the killer is certainly more likely to be Captain Carou."

As the black and white police car passed the railroad station for the third time, Elliott said, "If he were smart, of course...the killer is most likely Captain Carou. At least we should look at him first."

Why do both detectives lean toward blaming Captain Carou?

Answer on page 94.

Elliott Finds a Clue

Officer Alvin Boysenberry was nervous. He had lost track of Detective Elliott Savant—"momentarily," he had reported to headquarters—three hours ago. Now they were both supposed to be here at the home of Dave and Sharon Allenwrench investigating a burglary. Boysenberry was quite unsettled because his job was to keep track of the elusive detective so that he did not get lost. It was never explained to him why Detective Savant might get lost or what would be so terrible if he did. It was just his job to see that it didn't happen. Fortunately, Sergeant Rebekah Shurshot was there interviewing Sharon and Dave, so Boysenberry had time to pace back and forth and fret until he heard the familiar rumble of Elliott's Harley Davidson motorcycle.

Elliott walked into the house wearing his usual trench

coat and galoshes, but what caught the eye first, of course, was the black helmet with the decorative plume of colorful feathers sticking up nearly a foot from the center of the helmet. Elliott said the bright orange, yellow, and purple feathers added visibility and made it safer for him to drive his motorcycle.

Dave and Sharon, the young couple who sat on the flowered couch across from Sergeant Shurshot, had a lot to talk about. They were new to town. They had been warmly welcomed to the neighborhood. They had been invited to join a local church. But they did not feel so welcome right now. They had been robbed before they'd even unpacked all their boxes.

"Sharon went to the grocery store with our neighbors," Dave explained. "I thought she was in the bedroom unpacking. So when I went to the hardware store to get some things, I didn't bother to lock the doors."

Sharon said, "When I got home, the place was a mess."

"At least we didn't have to empty the boxes," Dave said. "They were dumped out all over the house."

Elliott appreciated Dave's sense of humor in the situation, but no one laughed.

Sharon continued: "The burglars went through everything. They took jewelry that really didn't amount to much, but they also took an envelope from our bedroom that had money we had brought to open our new bank account. We closed our bank account back home, and we foolishly brought the money in cash."

"Even more foolish was the fact that we put off opening a new account. We should never have left that much money lying around the house," Dave said.

"It is all gone," Sharon said. "The burglars even got into the refrigerator. They ate sandwiches. It looks like they even watched television while they had a little lunch. They even took a bite out of a block of cheese in the refrigerator. It's still there!"

"Our neighbor did see a black pickup truck in our driveway. She thought it was ours or movers or something," Dave said.

"Do we have any suspects, yet?" Elliott asked Sergeant Shurshot.

"Good news and bad news," Sergeant Shurshot said. "There have been other break-ins in the area. We have an idea who's been doing it."

"That's the good news?" Elliott said.

"Right," Sergeant Shurshot said. "You can guess the bad news—no proof and no new evidence."

"I think we actually have both right here," Elliott said. "I think I smell a rat."

What was Elliott talking about?

Answer on page 93.

Sliver Slips

"Sliver Shank is one wily hombre we won't have to worry about. Somebody finally caught up with him," Officer Boysenberry announced to the group of police officers and detectives who stood in front of a small isolated house on a country road. The name on the mailbox was "S. Shank."

"So you think this is his blood?" Dr. Quicksolve said, pointing to the trail of blood that led from the living room carpet out the front door and then out to the edge of the road. There was no body.

"He could be right," Officer Beekerjar said. "We can test this blood."

"Well, for quite some time, he's slipped past us and other police departments, leaving a trail of crime clear across the state," Sergeant Rebekah Shurshot said. She took off her blue cap and wiped her forehead. "He's always gotten away, leaving behind so many false clues that it was hard to know where to begin. Though I have to admit, it's hard to believe he could really come to an end so easily."

"Well, from the mess in the house and this trail of smeared blood, it doesn't look like he came to an end easily," Beekerjar said. "It definitely looks like someone was murdered in the house and his body was dragged out the front door to the road where it was taken away in the trunk of a car or something."

"The problem is the lack of a body," Dr. Quicksolve said.

As the discussion was going on, the lanky Detective Elliott Savant was standing at the edge of the road with his face pressed into the mailbox. It looked like the mailbox had sprouted wild, black, curly hair, or some strange bird had built a nest inside it.

Elliott straightened up and called Officer Beekerjar. Then he pointed to the base of the post the mailbox sat on. When they walked back to the group, Beekerjar was holding something in the palm of his hand.

"What is that?" Sergeant Shurshot asked.

"It looks like fibers from a rope," Beekerjar said.

"Someone probably used a rope to drag the post over there," Sergeant Shurshot said. "Or to straighten it," she added.

"There were marks on the post like rope burns," Beekerjar said.

Elliott walked into the house. He walked back out, following the trail left by the body that had been dragged across the yard.

"I don't think he's dead," Elliott said. "I think he just wants us to think he's dead."

Boysenberry laughed. "So you think he stabbed or bludgeoned or shot himself, and then he dragged himself out of the house and across the lawn so we would think he was dead and stop looking for him?" he asked.

"Something like that," Elliott said.

How could Sliver do that?

Answer on page 90.

Halloween Escape

Strange things happen on Halloween—not because of goblins and ghouls, but because people do strange things.

The Men's State Facility was hauntingly quiet. It sat out in the middle of a large, dark field, surrounded by bright lights and a 15-foot fence. Spiraling barbed wire glistened under the lights, adding a special eeriness to the gloomy setting.

Out beyond the prison, on all four sides, lay pitch-black darkness. They walked in three lines that stretched from one corner of the prison fence to the other on the south side. There was a low rumbling hum as they approached from the darkness. There were two guards in each of the two watchtowers on the corners of the huge silver fence.

The attention of all four men was focused on the approaching army of little witches, clowns, animals, and ghouls. As they drew ever closer, the guards were gradually able to understand what they heard. "Trick or treat! Trick or treat! Trick or treat! Trick or treat!" It sounded like the voices of children, but the clocklike precision and the perfect cadence was unsettling, frightening.

The incredulous guards watched silently as nearly a hundred children approached the tall, electrified fence of the maximum-security prison. The guards suddenly began grabbing phones and shouting into them. Sirens blared. Lights flashed. They could only watch as the first row hit the fence before the electricity could be turned off. The explosion of sparks, fire, and the sudden stream of black smoke did not even slow down the second wave of trick-or-treaters as they piled into the burning shards in front of them. Then the third line came, never stopping, never slowing, never missing a step. The electricity was off by now, but the third line of little people seemed intent on marching right through the fence.

It took several minutes before anyone got down to the carnage to discover that the army of trick-or-treaters were not kids at all, but little wheeled robots in Halloween costumes.

It took nearly half an hour to do a count of the prisoners and find out one had somehow escaped. A convicted killer, Thurston Drinker, was free.

What was assumed to be the dark sedan that had been seen speeding away from the prison fence, a rental car as it turned out, was found at a small airport nearby. An airplane had been stolen. It was found at another small airport a hundred miles away. This time, a helicopter had been stolen. It was found on a secluded beach, where a yacht had been stolen. Only parts of the yacht were found, but the search continued.

That was why Detective Elliott Savant was floating out on Lake Michigan in a large donut-shaped inner tube among the debris of the yacht, which, Officer Beekerjar explained, had been blown up in some kind of explosion in the engine compartment.

Detective Savant paddled over to the Coast Guard boat, where two police officers pulled him up and aboard.

"There's no sign of life. Drinker and his accomplices either died in the explosion or drowned," Lieutenant Rootumout said.

"Well," Elliott said, drying himself with a large towel, "it's too cold to enjoy a swim."

"It's too cold to survive very long," Officer Beekerjar said.

"What have we found?" Elliott asked.

"We've found life vests, cushions from the cabin, pieces of the yacht, and we also found a set of brand new luggage filled with a man's clothing. The suitcases are marked 'T. Drinker' in gold letters. We got him all right!" Lieutenant Rootumout said.

"No," Elliott said. "He got away."

Why did Elliott think Thurston Drinker got away?

Answer on page 92.

Answers

Jump Rope (Page 22)—Dr. Quicksolve knew that someone working alone late at night in a large building would probably lock the doors after everyone left so something like this wouldn't happen. He also knew that for safety reasons (in case of fire, etc.) school doors have a crash-bar that lets you exit even if the door is locked. A robber most likely wouldn't have been able to go out the front door and lock Jake in the hallway!

Chalk Snake (Page 39)—Miss Match did just what you would expect. She never changed her tone or interrupted her lesson for a second. She calmly picked up the snake as she continued talking about the Roman phalanx, walked to the window, which she pulled up with one hand, and dropped the snake to the grass three stories below. She continued her lesson and never mentioned the snake. There was no sound from the class.

The Bike in the Bushes (Page 31)—It looked like a typical thief's drop. The man could have stolen the bike and driven out toward the countryside, where he would toss the bike into the bushes. It could be a prearranged spot, or he could have been on a cell phone with an accomplice. The point was for the thief, who might have been seen, to get rid of the stolen item as soon as possible. If a witness described his van, the police might catch up to him quickly. His accomplice, in another vehicle, could just claim he'd found the bike and was going to try to find the owner. The accomplice must have been almost right behind the thief in this case. When it looked like there was no one around, he quickly drove up and took the bike while the boys were in the house!

Gunshots in the Night (Page 8)—Dr. Quicksolve figured the taxis kept going forward just as shots were fired and returning to do the whole thing again because they were filming a scene for a movie. Later, they found out he was right!

Sliver Slips (Page 82)—Sliver could have had blood drawn a little at a time to leave at the scene. He knew tests could prove it was his blood. Then he could have used a rope wrapped around the mailbox post to drag himself out the door, down the steps, and out to the road, leaving other clues for the forensic technicians to find as evidence that he was dragged across the lawn. Convincing the police that they should stop looking for him would be worth the pain of dragging himself around with a rope!

Portage Lake Burglar (Page 64)—Elliott used his jack-knife to mark the soles of the suspect's shoes so they could identify him as the burglar the next time he left tracks at a burglary site.

Rescue Dog (Page 10)—The name is "Help!"

Panic for Donuts (Page 51)—"Water," Elliott said. "Direct your horse into water, and then you could just swim away!"

"Good idea," Junior said, "if your feet don't get caught in the stirrups."

"I wonder if you could make saddles that float like airline cushions," Elliott mused.

"Well, now we know what to do," Junior said. "Let's eat!"

"Yes," Flora said. "Pack a snorkel in your saddlebag just in case!"

"And flippers!" Fauna said.

Laughing Matters (Page 24)—Both vehicles should have a remote electric garage door opener in them that could be used to open the garage.

Second—With their hands in front of them and another rope around their waists, it should be easy for them to untie each other.

Third—a garage door usually has a cord hanging down so you can open it even if the electricity fails. They could probably have reached it without even untying the ropes.

Fourth—They could just turn off the engine and wait for help.

Cardigan (Page 16)—If a cardigan sweater was unbuttoned, it would fly up along the sides of the man running away, and it would be easy to tell if it were a cardigan sweater—even from behind!

Sergeant Shurshot Solves a Case (Page 28)—Sergeant Shurshot remembered the cats and how the cat hair had clung to her uniform. If the jogging outfit belonged to Malisha Demone, it would have cat hair on it from her two cats. The hair could be matched to the two cats, supporting the picture evidence that the outfit had belonged to Malisha!

No Germs Allowed (Page 41)—Knowing that Skeeter was sick and seeing how crisp his homework was (and, of course, knowing Miss Match), Junior quickly figured out that Miss Match had put Skeeter's papers in her oven to kill the germs!

The General's Last Stop (Page 73)—The fact that the sergeant wore boots with laces doesn't mean they were only available to him. The captain could have been the one with the bomb and gas mask. He could have taken the laces from the sergeant's boots, killed the general, and replaced the laces before the sergeant revived!

Also, the general must have had a pair of shoes with laces somewhere. Actually, any lacelike cord could have been used and discarded from the train. This case could not be solved so easily.

Hit-and-Run (Page 12)—The man said he had gone to Slippery Oliver's Oil and Lube. Those places usually put a sticker on the windshield to tell when you had your oil change and when to come back. Dr. Quicksolve saw a sticker, but it indicated that the last oil change was weeks ago, not that day!

Halloween Escape (Page 85)—Elliott thought from the beginning the trail was too easy to follow—car to airplane to helicopter to boat. But the clincher was the new luggage. An escaped convict wouldn't buy luggage clearly giving away his identity!

Jocko (Page 36)—Prissy explained that if people were willing to help others escape slavery, they would tie a green ribbon on Jocko's arm if it was safe for escaped slaves to approach the house at that time. If it was dangerous at that time, they would tie a red ribbon as a warning. The mystery is that more people don't learn about this when they study American history!

Elliot Finds a Clue (Page 79)—Elliott figured the cheese with a bite taken out of it would be great evidence. The burglar left his unique set of teeth prints, which could be matched to the suspect!

Jekyll Tries to Hide (Page 44)—Elliott and Dr. Quicksolve figured Jekyll could have used his garage door opener to signal another remote control he had his accomplices hide in the tree down the block, which signaled another control on the corner, which signaled another one around the corner, etc., until signals got to the bomb on the podium. That way, Jekyll could be away from the scene with an alibi and still detonate the bomb!

Terry Taggert's Terrible Day (Page 19)—If Turk bought a new bowling ball to use as a crystal ball, he wouldn't have had any finger holes drilled into it. On the other hand, Tina, a professional bowler, would have had finger holes drilled in the ball precisely to fit her hand, probably for a special grip!

Across a Crowded Room (Page 67)—Actually, Detective Elliott Savant did not arrest the officers. He arrested Martha Peterson because she knew the crackers were poisoned before she could have learned about the lab report.

Stealing Bases/Stealing Cars (Page 59)—Elliott knew that the shortstop, number six, who had hit the ball late to the opposite field down the first base line, was right-handed. He knew number sixteen, the first baseman who batted from the first base side of the plate, was left-handed. If Officer Longarm could not reach the carjacker's gun hand, the thief must have been right-handed. So it must have been the shortstop, number six!

If He Were Smart... (Page 76)—Since the killer knew the two of them would be the only suspects, he would try to do something to make investigators think the other one was the guilty person. That implies he would not use something like a shoelace if he were the only person wearing shoelaces at the time. So the best suspect for the moment was Captain Carou, who was wearing cowboy boots with no laces...if he were smart!

Guards (Page 56)—Donkeys do keep coyotes away from their own family. If there were only one donkey, he might "adopt" the goats as his family and protect them.

(This is what really happened!)

Read Other
Quicksolve Mysteries™

This is the eighth book in the ongoing series of Dr. Quicksolve mini-mysteries. You can order these books from your bookstore. Here is a list of other Quicksolve books written by Jim Sukach and published by Sterling:

Quicksolve Whodunit Puzzles

Baffling Whodunit Puzzles

Challenging Whodunit Puzzles

Great Quicksolve Whodunit Puzzles

Clever Quicksolve Whodunit Puzzles

Crime-Scene Whodunit Puzzles

Wicked Whodunits

Index